DRACULA

BRAM STOKER

www.realreads.co.uk

Retold by Chaz Brenchley
Illustrated by Vanessa Lubach

Published by Real Reads Ltd
Stroud, Gloucestershire, UK
www.realreads.co.uk

First published in 2008
Reprinted 2011

ISBN 978-1-906230-16-6

Printed in China by Wai Man Book Binding (China) Ltd
Designed by Lucy Guenot
Typeset by Bookcraft Ltd, Stroud, Gloucestershire

CONTENTS

THE CHARACTERS

Count Dracula

A mysterious aristocrat in a distant castle. But who – or what – is he really?

Jonathan Harker

A young solicitor, trapped in a terrifying adventure. Will his courage see him through?

Mina Harker

Jonathan's new wife.
Will a simple holiday with her friend Lucy doom them both?

Professor Van Helsing

He may be the wisest man in Europe, but can his wisdom save his friends?

Lucy Westenra

Two good men are in love with her, but will she be seduced by something darker?

Doctor Seward

Lucy's rejected suitor. Does he love her enough to fight for her life?

Dracula's brides

Can Jonathan resist the dangerous attraction of these beautiful but evil women? Will they obey Count Dracula?

DRACULA

FROM JONATHAN HARKER'S JOURNAL

6th May: Castle Dracula

The count's carriage met me, by arrangement, at the Borgo Pass. I had come this far on the public coach, after long weary days by boat and train through lands that were ever less familiar. My companions on the coach seemed almost like medieval peasants, as though I had travelled in time as well as in space. They were superstitious brutes; when I mentioned my destination they crossed themselves, and one hung a crucifix round my neck.

It was already dark when we came to the pass. There was no immediate sign of another carriage. I thought we were early, but our driver cried, 'He is not here! He will not come tonight!'

Before he could whip his horses on, they began to kick and plunge wildly, so that he had to rein them in again. There were hoofbeats on the road, startled screams from the peasants. A carriage drawn by four magnificent coal-black horses drew up beside us. The driver was a tall man with a large hat hiding his face. I could see only his eyes, which glowed red in the lamplight.

He took my luggage, and helped me into the carriage with a steely grip. A moment later we swept away, into the darkness of the pass.

Howling followed us, like a chorus on the wind. Then it was all around us. Our horses shivered and reared in the traces; the driver needed all his strength to control them.

We took a bend – and there sat a wolf, stock-still in the road. Nothing could have forced those horses past him. They stood and trembled; one screamed with fright. As if that were a summons, a ring of wolves suddenly

encircled us with white teeth and lolling tongues, terrible in their grim silence.

The driver rose in his seat and spoke a word of imperious command. At the same time he swung his arms, as though to brush the pack aside. A cloud passed across the moon; when I could see again, the roadway was clear.

On and on we drove, higher and higher into the mountains, until we came into the courtyard of a ruined castle. No light shone in the tall windows, and the broken battlements made a jagged line against the stars.

The driver helped me alight, and handed down my bags. Then he shook the reins and left me standing before a great door studded with ancient nails.

There was no bell or knocker, and no point in shouting through thick stone walls. I waited, wondering – not for the first time – quite how I, a young English solicitor, had found myself caught up in such a grim adventure.

At last I heard footsteps beyond the door, and the clank of massive bolts drawn back. A key grated in the lock, and the door swung open.

Within stood a tall old man with a long white moustache, clad from head to foot in black.

'Welcome to my house. Enter freely and of your own will.'

He shook my hand; his was as cold as ice, and as strong as the driver's. I wondered briefly if they were the same person.

'Count Dracula?'

He bowed, and lifted my luggage himself. I protested – surely he had servants? – but he insisted, leading me up a broad staircase. We came to a warm and well-lit suite of rooms, where supper was laid out ready for me. He himself would not eat, but he kept me company until I was satisfied. It was now so late that the first streaks of dawn were showing through the window. Wolves howled again on the slopes below, and the count's eyes gleamed.

'Listen to them – the children of the night. What music they make!'

When he smiled, I saw with a shudder that his teeth were peculiarly sharp.

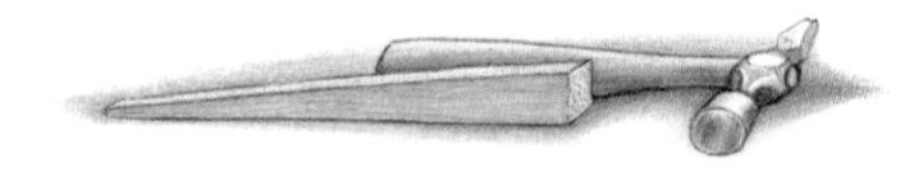

7th May

I slept late, and woke to find a meal laid out for me but the castle apparently empty. There was no sign of the count, nor of any servants. I could not find a mirror anywhere, so had to use my own little travelling-glass to shave and brush my hair.

I did not like to explore too far without the count's consent, so I was glad to find a library, with many books in English. I was still there when the count appeared.

'These books are my friends,' he said. 'Through these, I have learned to love your England. Now, through your goodness,

I will come to live in London. You will tell me all about this house you have found for me. I trust you will stay a while, and correct me when I make an error in the English language. I have learned it only through these books, and never had the chance to speak it before.'

I assured him that his English was excellent, and promised to stay as long as I could.

'Go anywhere you wish within my castle,' he said, 'except where the doors are locked. Now, tell me of the house in London.'

The London property was a large old house set in its own grounds, behind a high stone wall. I fetched the plans and deeds, and he asked a great many questions. We talked all night, and again I did not come to bed until cock-crow.

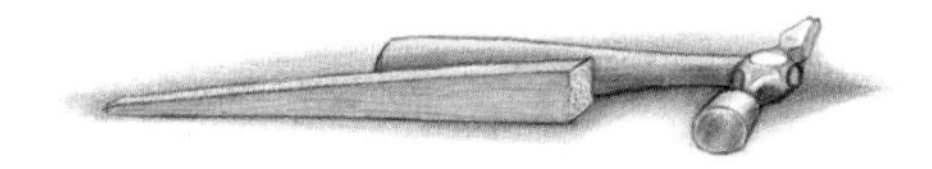

8th May

Today I hung my little mirror in the window, and had just begun to shave when I heard the count say 'Good morning.'

I started, and cut myself with the razor. The mirror reflected the whole room, but I had not seen him approach. I glanced back, and there he was. I looked in the mirror – but he had no reflection!

When I turned to face him, he saw the blood on my face. His eyes blazed with a demonic fury, and he lunged for my throat. I jerked away; his hand touched the string of my crucifix, and his mood changed in a moment.

'Take care,' he said, 'how you cut yourself. It is more dangerous than you think.' Then he seized my mirror, crying, 'This is the wretched mischief-maker! Away with it!'

He flung it out of the window, and I heard it shatter in the courtyard far below.

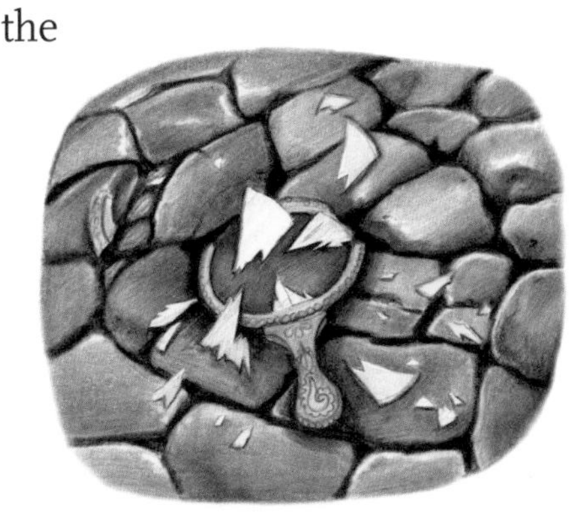

The count left me to breakfast alone. He is a most peculiar man; I have never yet seen him eat or drink anything.

After the meal, I explored as much of the castle as I could. It stands on the very edge of a precipice, above a terrible fall. The views are magnificent – but I tried door after door, and found them all locked against me. The windows above that dreadful drop are the only way out of here. I am a prisoner!

There is no point complaining to the count. It is he who turns the keys against me.

Before dinner I spied through a crack in the door and saw him lay the table himself. It is as I suspected; there are no servants here. He must have been the carriage-driver too, the man who could command the wolves. No wonder the peasants are so afraid of him. So, now, am I.

Nevertheless, I had a long talk with him after dinner. He spoke of his family pride, and the turbulent history of this land. So vividly does he describe the past, one could almost believe that he had been there. He said that he hoped I would stay a month. I could find no way to refuse. I cannot even write an honest letter to my beloved Mina, because I have no way to send it except via the count, and I am convinced that he would read it.

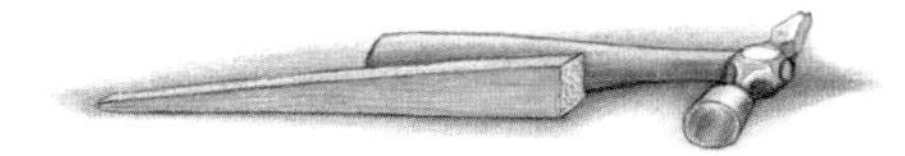

16th May

I was in my room, leaning out of the window, when my eye caught something moving below. It was the count, emerging from a window and crawling down the wall, head first like a lizard. What manner of man is this?

Searching the castle desperately in his absence, I found one door unlocked. It led to rooms that were shabby and dusty, but somehow comforting after the gloom and dread of my own chambers.

I lay on an ancient couch, and must have fallen asleep. When I awoke, I was not alone. Three young women stood in the moonlight, whispering together. They cast no shadows. Their brilliant white teeth shone like pearls against their ruby lips.

'You first,' one said. 'He is young and strong; there will be kisses for us all.'

The blonde one stepped forward, licking her lips like an animal. I felt those lips touch my throat, then two sharp teeth. I waited, with desire and terror intimately mixed.

At the last moment, the count burst in upon us. A fierce sweep of his arm hurled the young woman from me.

'How dare you touch him? Any of you?

This man belongs to me!'

'You promised him to us!'

'When I am done with him,' the count growled, 'you may kiss him at your will. Now go!'

'Are we to have nothing tonight?' I could not tell which of the women spoke; it might have been all of them together, like some ghastly chorus.

The count gestured towards a sack he had tossed upon the floor. When they ripped it open I heard the low wail of a terrified child. Then the women and the sack were simply gone, fading into the moonlight.

The horror overcame me, and I sank into unconsciousness.

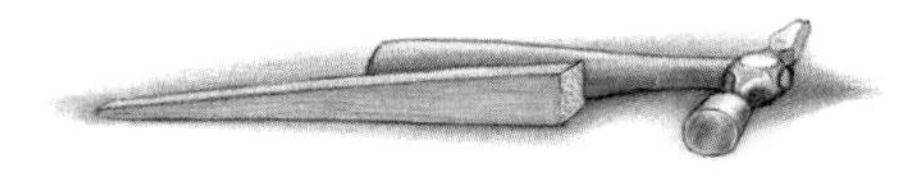

17th May

I woke in my own bed, where the count must have carried me. I am in a fever of anxiety now, for he knows that I have seen too much. Every minute I hear the echo of that poor lost child's terror in my mind. It is too late for him. If I linger, it will be too late for me. I must escape!

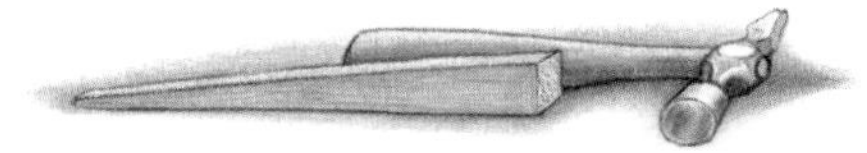

I am not sure what the date is. It has been days since I wrote in my journal: helpless days, hopeless days. The doors are always locked.

There have been wagons in the courtyard below, fetching in great wooden boxes, but the gypsies who drive them serve the count; they will not take a letter for me. What does he mean to carry in such vast crates?

I have rarely seen the count by daylight. Perhaps he is a true nocturnal. If I slip into his room, perhaps I can find the keys and free myself while he sleeps. The door is always locked, but there is another way. He himself climbs in and out through the windows of this appalling place. Where one man can, so can another. I will try it, at least. If I die trying, I am no worse off.

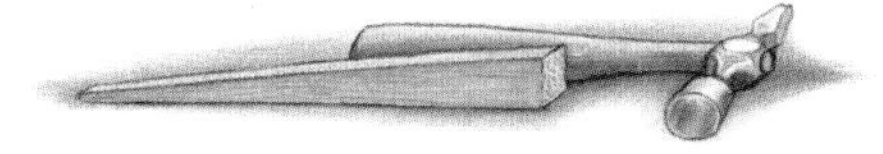

Later

I am safely back, although the climb is dreadful. The stones of the wall are large and rough, giving plenty of handholds; it is the height which preys on the mind. Still, I made my way down to the count's window. His room was blessedly empty. I looked for keys, but found none.

A door in one corner took me down a circular stairway to an old ruined chapel, where all the floor had been dug up and the soil placed in those great wooden boxes. In one of them, on a pile of freshly-turned earth, lay the count! His eyes and cheeks held no sign of death, yet I could see no sign of breath in him. I would have

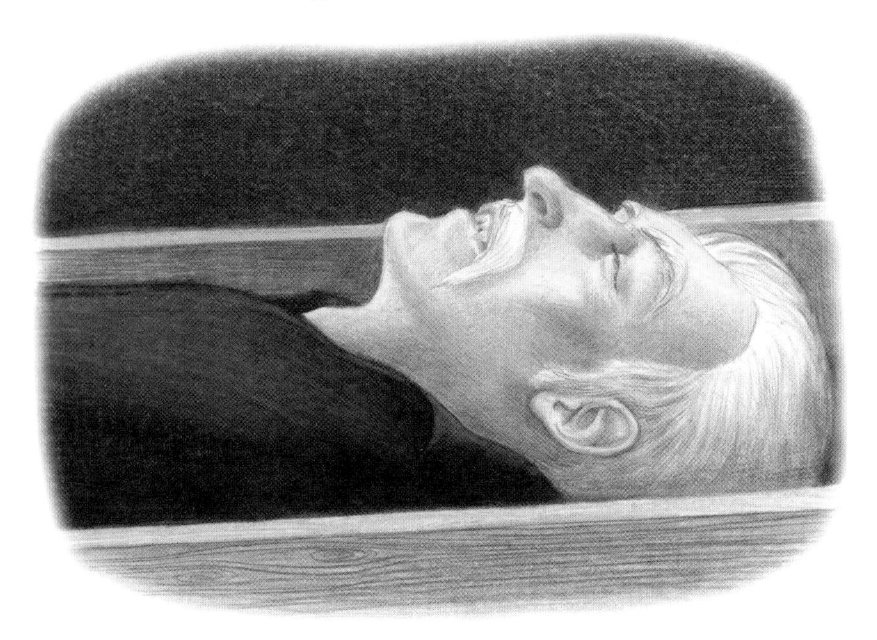

searched his clothes for keys, but there was such hate emanating from his unconscious body, I fled that place and made the desperate climb back to my own room.

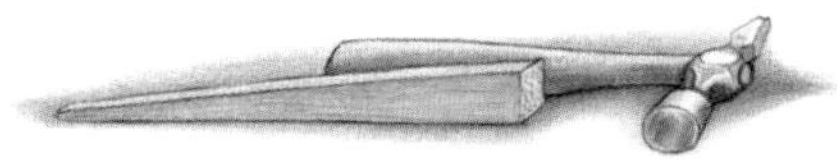

Next evening

Today I saw the count go and come again with another writhing sack, some miserable child stolen from its parents. Later I heard a whispering at my door, the count's voice: 'Go, back to your own place! Tomorrow night, he is yours!'

There was a low cold laughter, and when I flung open the door I saw the three terrible young women licking their lips. They laughed again, horribly, and ran away.

I dare not stay here another day. Come what may, I must escape or fall.

I climbed out of my window again, and down to the count's room. I knew where to find the monster: down the winding stair, in the old chapel.

There was the great box, the lid not yet nailed down. I lifted it up, and my soul thrilled with horror. The count's white hair and moustache had changed to iron-grey; he looked halfway to being young again! His flesh was bloated, and fresh blood trickled from the corners of his mouth.

I had no weapon, but a shovel lay nearby. I seized that, and swung the sharp edge of it at the hateful face. As I did so, his head turned, and his eyes blazed at me. I was paralysed by

that basilisk stare; the shovel twisted in my weakened grip, and did no more than gash his forehead.

The lid fell down again, and the last I saw of him was his dreadful, bloodstained grin.

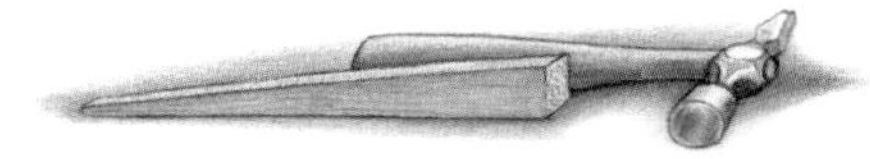

In the distance I can hear voices, the crack of whips, the rumble of wagon-wheels. Men are coming, to take his box and the others. I have run back up to the count's room, but there is no shelter here. I barely have time to write these words. If the men do not find me, the devil-women will. Faugh! I will not wait for them. I will climb down from the window here. The precipice is steep; either I will escape to my Mina, or fall and die a man. If I am found, this story will be found with me. Farewell!

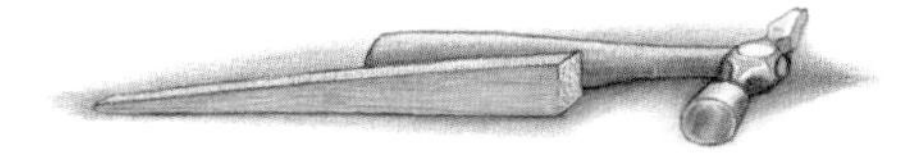

FROM MINA HARKER'S JOURNAL

I am staying in Whitby, with my dear friend Lucy Westenra. Her poor ailing mother has died at last, but Lucy is uplifted now, having been proposed to twice in a single day! She turned down the good Dr Seward and said yes to her beloved Arthur, which makes me almost as happy as it has him. I understand that the young men are now firm friends. Men are very strange.

A church here stands on a cliff above the town, with a graveyard that runs right to the cliff's edge. It is my favourite place to sit. I come

up often with Lucy, or on my own when I am sad and worried, as I am now.

I have had no news from my husband Jonathan. It is most unlike him to neglect me in this way. I cannot help but feel anxious when he is far away in a strange land.

Closer to hand, I am worried also about Lucy, who is sleepwalking again, as she used to when she was a little girl. I must remember to lock our door at night.

Today I was quite frightened by an old man who declared that something in the wind smelled like death. It was a relief when the coastguard came by. He says there is a storm coming. We could see a ship far out behaving very strangely. She steered this way and that, as the wind and waves took her. I think he is anxious for her safety if she doesn't put in before the storm hits. Her danger put my own worries to shame, they seem so petty – but oh, how I wish that Jonathan would write!

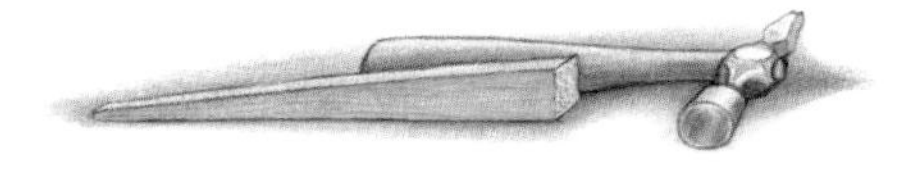

9th August

The storm broke last night, in a terrible tempest. The coastguard was right to worry about that Russian ship; she was blown directly into harbour, and beached below the cliffs. They say an immense dog leapt from the bows the instant she struck, and disappeared into the night. If that is the strangest part of the story, it is not the most terrible. They found a

dead seaman lashed to the wheel, with a rosary in his hands – and not a soul else on board!

Her cargo was apparently no more than a number of wooden boxes, filled with soil. Those have already been claimed, and transported away.

People are saying that the ship's log records the mysterious disappearance one by one of the entire crew, since they took the cargo

aboard at Varna. It also records rumours of a stowaway, a stranger seen in glimpses. It all sounds quite mad – and yet, the crew is gone. Whitby is alive with speculation.

The log makes no mention of the dog. Nor has it been seen ashore since that night. Perhaps it was a mirage of night and storm. But a coal merchant's mastiff, a large and fierce animal itself, was found dead this morning with its throat torn out.

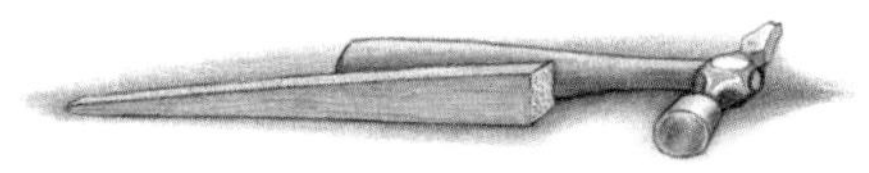

11th August

Such a terrible adventure! I woke in the middle of the night, and Lucy was not in her bed. I thought I had locked the door, but it stood open. When I had searched the house, I dressed hurriedly and went out. There was a flutter of white on the cliff path. I climbed in pursuit, and saw a figure half-reclining on our favourite bench – but something dark bent

over it. Man or beast, I could not tell. I called Lucy's name and saw a pale face rise, with red gleaming eyes.

I shrieked and ran to her, and found her quite alone. She breathed in gasps, and in her sleep she shuddered, and drew her nightdress tight about her throat. It took an age to wake her, and she seemed so cold I fastened my own shawl around her with a pin. I must have been clumsy with it, because when I finally had her safe back in our room, I found two pinpricks of blood on her neck.

13th August

We are having quiet days, but disturbed nights. I wake to find Lucy struggling with the locked door, or else fast asleep but sitting up and pointing at the window, where a great bat flutters. When I hurry to draw the curtains, it flies away across the harbour.

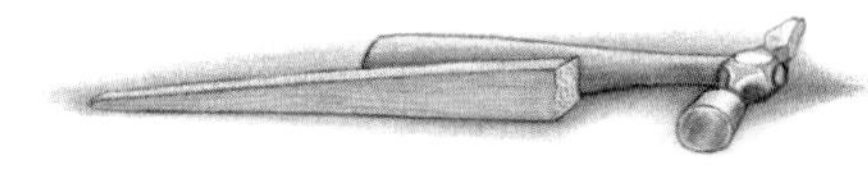

14th August

Walking along the cliff, Lucy murmured, 'His red eyes.' Startled, I saw that she was looking half-dreamily at our bench, where a dark figure sat. For a moment I thought he had eyes of flame, but it was only a reflection of the sunset.

Later, I went out alone, to hide my increasing anxiety about Jonathan. Coming back, I saw Lucy in our window and waved, but she seemed to be asleep. Strangely, I thought there was a bird on the ledge beside her. When I came up to the room she was just going to bed, still apparently asleep, with a hand pressed to her throat, as if she were cold or frightened in her dream.

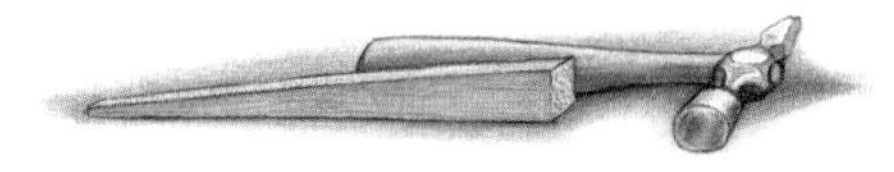

17th August

I do not understand Lucy's fading condition. She eats well, goes to bed early and sleeps late; and yet she is pale and haggard, languid, weaker day by day. Those tiny wounds the pin made in her throat have not healed. If anything, they seem larger.

19th August

Joy, joy! Though it is tempered by worry. I have news of my dear Jonathan! He has been dreadfully ill, raving of blood and demons, but he is mending now, under the care of the good nuns of Budapest. I am leaving at once to nurse him and bring him home. I dislike leaving Lucy when she is not well herself, but my husband must come first. She will have her own beloved Arthur to watch over her; his home is in London, but he has been sent for and is expected tomorrow.

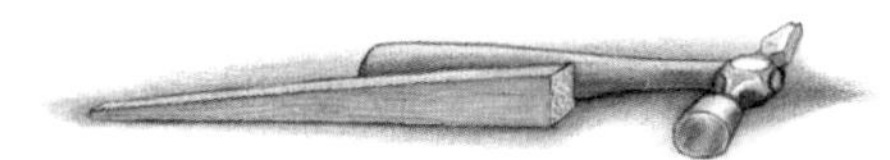

FROM DR SEWARD'S JOURNAL

2nd September

I have been summoned from London to Whitby by Arthur Holmwood, my rival – my successful rival! – for the love of Lucy Westenra. He is most anxious about her. Having seen her, so am I. She is woefully different from when I last saw her: pale and bloodless, sleepwalking at night and exhausted in the day. I am baffled, and can give Arthur no reassurance.

I have written to my old friend and master, Professor Van Helsing. He is a philosopher and a scientist, and knows more obscure medicine than any man I could name. He says he will come as soon as he can.

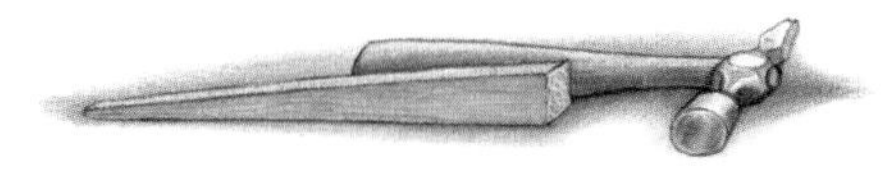

6th September

Lucy was so much worse today, pale as chalk and her breathing painful to hear. Thank God,

Van Helsing has arrived. One look, and he said, 'There is no time to be lost, or she will die from sheer want of blood. She must have a transfusion!'

Arthur insisted that it be his blood we gave her. I watched the colour come back to Lucy's cheeks, as it faded from Arthur's. While Van Helsing was detaching his equipment, I heard him hiss in alarm. There are two puncture-wounds on her throat, which she had kept hidden under a velvet band.

'Is this how she lost so much blood?' I demanded.

'Her bed would have been drenched scarlet. And yet ... I must go back to Amsterdam,' he said. 'When I return – well, we will see. Meantime, keep watch over her; do not sleep, and do not leave her alone!'

10th September

Lucy has seemed better day by day. Last night she would not let me sit up over her. She had a fire lit in the next room, with the door open between the two. I stretched out on the sofa, and – dog-tired as I was – I forgot all about everything.

Professor Van Helsing woke me this morning. I was delighted to see him, but when we went in to the patient, his gasp of horror chimed with mine. Lucy was more horribly white than ever, fainting and barely alive.

It was my turn to give her blood. When all was done, Van Helsing fetched a box of white garlic flowers and insisted in laying them all around the room, including in a wreath around Lucy's neck. I asked laughingly if this was a spell to keep out an evil spirit. 'Perhaps it is,' he said.

It is evening now, and she is sleeping peacefully. When I went in, I thought something flapped in fury at the window.

What does it all mean?

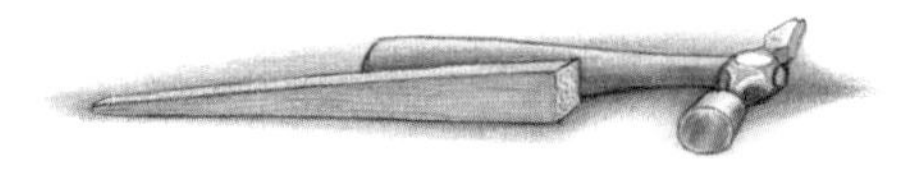

20th September

The news is almost too terrible to write. Lucy had seemed so much better, we let her sleep unwatched. This morning, we found that she had torn the garlic flowers from her throat, and she was too weak to wake. Her gums were white, and her teeth seemed longer than usual, and sharp.

Van Helsing was in despair. 'She cannot live,' he said.

He sent me to fetch Arthur. That unhappy young man knelt beside his love, and her eyes opened. 'Kiss me,' she entreated, in a soft voluptuous voice – but Van Helsing dragged him back, crying, 'Not for your life!'

A spasm of rage passed over Lucy's face; then her eyes closed, and all too soon her breathing ceased.

'She is dead,' Van Helsing said; 'but alas, it is not yet over. This is only the beginning.'

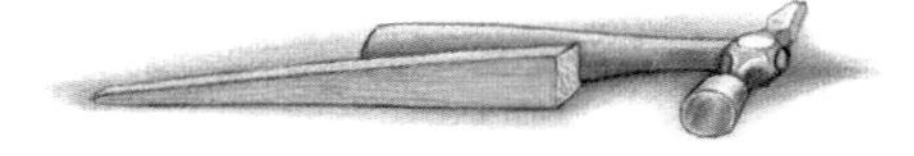

FROM MINA HARKER'S JOURNAL

22nd September

Walking down Piccadilly with Jonathan, I felt so glad to have him safe at last. He suddenly clutched my arm so tight it hurt me. He was very pale, and staring at a tall thin man with a black moustache and beard which made his teeth seem too white, too long.

'My God!' cried Jonathan. 'It is the man himself! The count! But he has grown young.'

And when we came home, there was a telegram to say that my dear Lucy is dead! God help us all to bear our troubles.

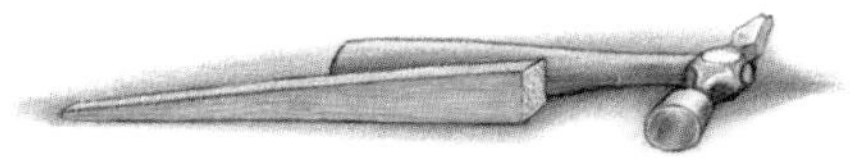

25th September

We have had a visit from a man called Van Helsing, who treated Lucy before her death. He wanted to know about her sleepwalking, so I gave him my diary to read. Then, because I trusted him and because I have been so worried about my husband, I gave him Jonathan's own strange record of his time at Castle Dracula.

Van Helsing assures me that it is no fancy of a disturbed mind. Every word of it is true! He clearly believes that Jonathan's story and Lucy's are linked together, though I cannot imagine how.

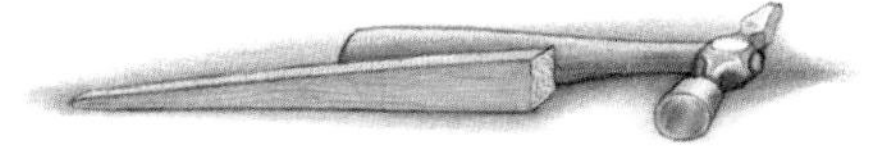

26th September: London

Van Helsing came today, to show me the evening paper: a story about children being tempted away by 'a beautiful lady', and found later with small puncture wounds at their throats.

'They sound just like Lucy's,' I said. 'Are you saying that these wounds were made the same way?'

'No,' he said solemnly, 'that they were made by Lucy herself!'

Any other man, I would have flung him from the house. I respect Van Helsing utterly, but this sounded mad. I said, 'We buried Lucy here in London, not a week ago.'

'Yes, and I want you to come with me now.'

'Where?'

'To her tomb!'

On the way, he talked of creatures that live on others' blood. For the first time I heard the word 'vampire'. It seemed all nonsense to me, until we entered poor Lucy's tomb by candlelight. Van Helsing opened her coffin – and her body was gone!

I was confused beyond measure, but he would not be questioned. 'We must tell her beloved Arthur,' he said. 'It is his right to know the truth, and see her put to rest.'

28th September

Tonight, the three of us held vigil outside the tomb. Towards dawn we saw a dim white figure with something in its arms. Moonlight showed us a woman, carrying a child. She came closer, and we saw a face we had once loved, Arthur and I – it was Lucy! And yet how changed, how cruel she seemed, her lips crimson with blood.

When she saw us, she snarled and flung the child aside; her eyes blazed with unholy light as she advanced on Arthur. 'Come to me, my love, and we can rest together.'

Her voice was diabolically sweet, and I thought Arthur would respond to it despite his horror. Van Helsing thrust himself between them, with a crucifix upheld. She recoiled from it and dashed into the tomb.

There was no more doubt in us. We took the child to safety, and agreed to meet again tomorrow, to do whatever must be done.

29th September

One more time, Van Helsing led us to the tomb. One more time, I saw the coffin opened. This time, Lucy's body was there – or a thing, rather, that inhabited her body, undead. She looked beautiful, and vile.

Van Helsing passed Arthur a hammer and a wooden stake.

'It must be you,' he said. 'While I read a prayer for the dead, place the stake over her heart and strike it through.'

When he struck, the thing in the coffin writhed and screeched. That lent him strength, I think, to strike again, until the heart was pierced.

Then she lay still, all foulness fled, in death our own sweet Lucy once again.

'Kiss her,' Van Helsing said, 'and bid her farewell. We will seal up the tomb and leave her to her rest. A greater task remains. We must seek the monster who brought this sorrow on you. I have clues to follow; we have another friend in this hunt. Will you promise to go on, to the bitter end?'

Each in turn, we took his hand and swore it.

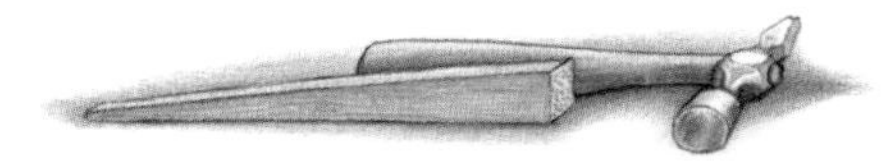

30th September

Mina Harker was our Lucy's finest friend; her husband Jonathan, it seems, can give a name to our enemy.

'Count Dracula is old,' Van Helsing said, 'centuries old; simple time cannot kill him. He can change his shape, to wolf or bat or mist. But still, he can be defeated. Garlic repels him, as does the crucifix. A stake through the heart will slay him; or cut off his head, even he cannot survive that. But first we have to find him.'

'He has bought a house,' Jonathan said, 'here in London. I know the address.'

Van Helsing warned us again how old and strong and cunning our adversary was. Nevertheless, we will seek out his house tomorrow, and destroy him if we can.

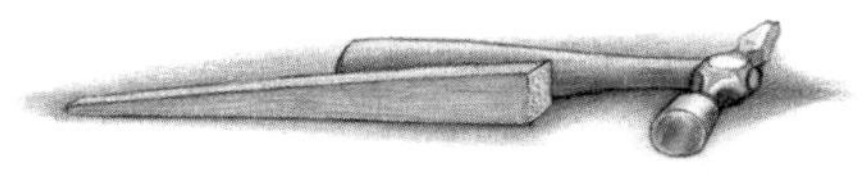

1st October

Jonathan led us to a big old house behind a high wall. Even in daylight it seemed webbed with shadow. Every window was closely shuttered; inside, we needed lamps.

In an otherwise empty room we found three great boxes. Jonathan shuddered; he had seen these in Castle Dracula, he said, filled with the foul earth of that place, and the count himself asleep in one of them.

We levered off their lids, and found a woman in each, ageless and perfect.

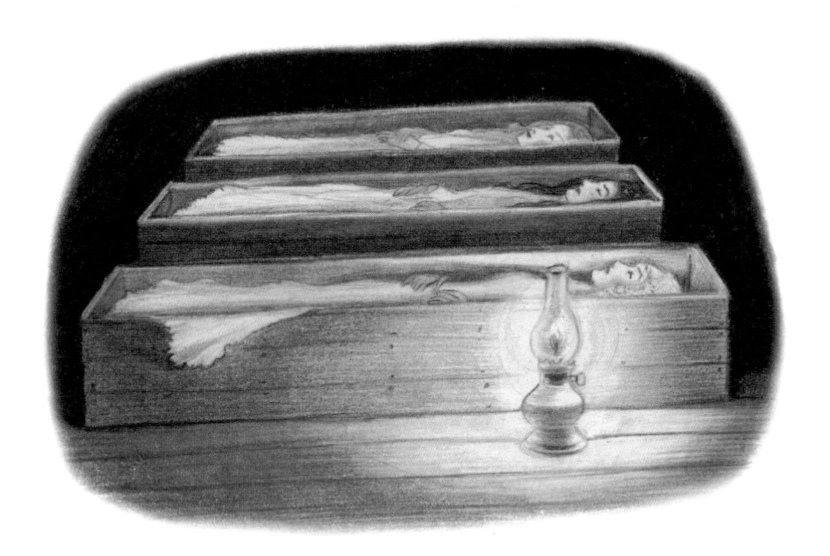

'They are beautiful,' I said, moved despite myself.

'They are sin itself!' cried Jonathan.

'Indeed,' Van Helsing said. 'Their flesh is uncorrupt, but I fear their souls were sold to that devil Dracula long ago.'

He produced hammer and stake and a heavy knife. It was butchers' work, and it needed all three of us to do it; one by one, we staked those dreadful women and cut away their heads, though they shrieked and fought like wild things from the first touch. Once they were safely dead, their bodies fell into vanishing dust.

We were still seeking their master. It took a while in that great dark tomb of a house, but we knew there had to be one more box of earth. Van Helsing says they need the soil of their own homeland to sleep in.

I glanced into a dark passage, and my heart stood still. For a moment I thought I saw the face of evil there, dreadfully pale, with burning red eyes. At the same time, I heard Jonathan gasp.

'I saw his face— !'

'So did I,' I said grimly, but we took our lamps down the passage and there was no one.

When we found the box at last, it was empty and the lid was off.

'He will come back,'

Van Helsing said, 'but when he does, this will be no comfort for him,' and he laid a crucifix in the box, to bless the earth and drive the vampire away.

We might have waited, but it was barely evening yet. He would not be likely to return before dawn; his kind do their worst work in the dark. I think we were all oppressed by that house, the knowledge of what we had done already and what we had yet to do.

Thus we chose not to wait, and thank god for that! Coming home in the dark, we found Mina already gone up to bed; but when Jonathan went to join her, the door to their room was locked from the inside.

He knocked and called, with no response. At last, he and I together put our shoulders to the door, and burst it in.

The monster was there, stooped over Mina where she knelt on the bed. Her white nightdress was stained with blood; his mouth

was red with it. He snarled at us like an animal; Van Helsing advanced, holding up his crucifix like a shield, and Dracula flinched. With one last gloating glance at Mina, he hurled himself through the window and was gone.

Jonathan ran to his wife, but Van Helsing cried, 'This is no time for comfort! Quickly now, quickly or we lose him!'

I was appalled, but in the cab, racing across London, Van Helsing explained himself. 'That devil has turned Mina, as he turned Lucy before her. She too will die and become as he is, unless we can slay him first. If he escapes us now, there will be no hope of that. Hurry!' he cried up to the cabman.

We came to the house, and hurtled in. I don't know what loathsome form the monster had taken on his own journey, but he had been too slow; we were there before him.

We waited in the room with his box, and soon heard a dreadful cry from below; he was here, and had found what we had done to his vicious women!

Slow, careful footsteps came along the hall; the count was expecting some surprise.

Suddenly he leaped into the room. An evil smile when he saw us, a cold stare of disdain that vanished as Jonathan slashed at him with the heavy knife he carried. Only his diabolical speed saved Dracula from that first stroke. His jump backwards brought him close to me;

I thrust my crucifix towards him, and rejoiced to see him cower. His eyes burned red with a baffled hatred as we drove him across the room to where Van Helsing waited with stake and hammer.

At the last moment, he tried again to dive for the window, but this time Jonathan was ready for him. This time, the blade of that great knife sheared through his throat. A moment later, the point of Van Helsing's stake pierced his heart, and all was done. Between one breath and the next, that ancient evil body crumbled into dust, freeing Mina and all of us and generations yet to come.

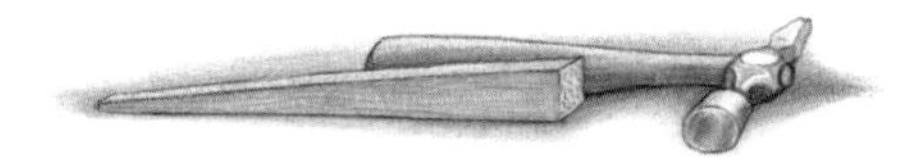

TAKING THINGS FURTHER

The real read

This *Real Read* version of *Dracula* is a retelling of Bram Stoker's magnificent work. If you would like to read the full novel in all its original horror, many complete editions are available, from bargain paperbacks to beautifully bound hardbacks. You will be able to find a copy in your local library or bookshop, or on the internet.

Filling in the spaces

The loss of so many of Bram Stoker's original words is a sad but necessary part of the shortening process. We have had to make some difficult decisions, omitting subplots and details, some important, some less so, but all interesting. We have also, at times, taken the liberty of combining two events into one, or of giving a character words or actions that originally belong to another. The points below will fill in some of the gaps, but nothing can beat the original.

- The original novel uses letters, telegrams and newspaper cuttings, as well as diary entries, to tell the story.

- In the original, fifty wooden boxes of earth are shipped to England, which Count Dracula intends to spread all around the country. One section of the novel involves the heroes tracking down those boxes one by one, until the count is cornered.

- The original Dr Seward runs a lunatic asylum, next door to the house that Count Dracula buys in London. The heroes use this as their base while they hunt the count and his boxes. One of Dr Seward's patients, Renfield, falls under the count's influence and admits him to the asylum, allowing him to attack Mina.

- In the original, Lucy actually receives three proposals in one day, not two. The third comes from a young American, Quincey Morris. She turns him down, of course, but he befriends both of her other suitors and remains very much part of the story, eventually dying in the final confrontation with Count Dracula.

- This retelling sets the confrontation in London. In the original, the count escapes the ambush and flees back to his castle in Transylvania, safe in the last of his boxes, which our heroes cannot catch up with before his ship sails. They give chase, tracking him through a telepathic connection that has existed between Mina and the count since he bit her. At last they overtake him in a gypsy convoy just before it reaches the castle, and slay him in his box while he sleeps.

- Dracula's three demon-women, his 'brides', do not come to England in the original novel. They remain in the castle, and our heroes find and destroy them there.

Back in time

The Victorian age was a time of great technological advances, where the scientific curiosity of earlier generations led to real-world applications, from the steam engine to electricity. It must have been an exciting time to live in, and Bram Stoker goes out of his way to portray some of that excitement.

The Victorians thought of themselves as great modernists, and *Dracula* is in many senses a modern novel. The original text is full of the innovations of the period, from the comparative ease of long-distance travel – just one generation earlier a solicitor would never have thought of travelling to Transylvania simply to complete a property sale – to electrical devices like the telegraph and the phonograph. It is very much a book about Jonathan and Mina's modern world meeting Count Dracula's ancient world, and only just winning through. In the end, even Van Helsing has to fall back on old-fashioned remedies – garlic, a crucifix and a sharp stake through the heart.

Bram Stoker derived his idea of a vampire from Eastern European folk tales and the popular romances of his own day. Like the science, though, much of what he used is genuine, and he actually invented very little. The Borgo Pass in Romania actually exists; close by is Bran Castle, where the real Vladislav Dracula was held prisoner for a time. He was a cruel man, also known as 'Vlad the Impaler'. His surname came from his father's title, *Dracul* or 'dragon'. Transylvania (the name means 'the land beyond the forests') was very little known at the time, and easy to romanticise. The Victorians were all too ready to believe that it was a country of medieval peasants and aristocratic overlords, haunted by superstition, very much in contrast to their own industry and rational understanding of the world.

Dracula was not the first bestseller about vampires. The first portrayal of a vampire as an aristocrat was John Polidori's *The Vampyre*, which used Lord Byron as its model. Sheridan LeFanu's *Carmilla* was another inspiration, and by the time *Dracula* was published in 1897 a number of other novels had been published in which the civilised world was threatened by fantastic creatures from primitive lands. The Victorians loved these stories, confident as they were that no such force could seriously threaten their empire.

Finding out more

We recommend the following books, websites and films:

Books

- Sheridan LeFanu, *Carmilla*, Prime Classics, 2000.
- Radu Florescu and Raymond McNally, *Dracula: His Life and Times*, Little, Brown, 2005.
- Barbara Belford, *Bram Stoker: A Biography*, Weidenfeld and Nicolson, 1996.
- Montague Summers, *The Vampire in Lore and Legend*, HarperCollins, 2001.
- Katherine Ramsland, *The Science of Vampires*, Berkley Publishing Group, 2002.
- Matthew Bunson, *The Vampire Encyclopedia*, Gramercy Books, 2001.

Websites

- www.ucs.mun.ca/~emiller/

Dracula's homepage – a general resource site for

information about Bram Stoker, *Dracula,* Vlad the Impaler and more.

- www.draculascastle.com/index3.html

A site promoting the real Transylvania.

- http://members.aol.com/johnfranc/draco5.htm

A biography of the man believed to be a model for Count Dracula, Vlad the Impaler.

- www.donlinke.com/drakula/vlad.htm

Another view of the original Count Dracula.

- http://vampires.monstrous.com

Monstrous Vampires – an encyclopaedia of vampires in fiction, film and myth.

Films

- *Bram Stoker's Dracula,* directed by Francis Ford Coppola, 1992. Despite the title it is not particularly faithful to the novel, but still beautiful to watch.
- *Dracula,* directed by Tod Browning, 1931. Starring Bela Lugosi, this is the film that defined our

idea of what a vampire should look like – evening dress, black hair brushed back from a widow's peak, clean-shaven – in direct contradiction to Bram Stoker's description in the novel.

- *Nosferatu,* directed by F. W. Murnau, 1929. A classic silent movie based on Stoker's novel.

- *Shadow of the Vampire,* directed by E. Elias Merhige, 2000. A movie about the making of *Nosferatu,* in which the star of that film turns out to be a genuine vampire himself ...

Food for thought

Here are some things to think about if you are reading *Dracula* alone, or ideas for discussion if you are reading it with friends.

In retelling *Dracula* we have tried to recreate, as accurately as possible, Bram Stoker's original plot and characters. We have also tried to imitate aspects of his style. Remember, however, that this is not the original work; thinking about the points below, therefore, can only help you begin to understand Stoker's craft. To move forward from here, turn to the full-length version of *Dracula* and lose yourself in his science and imagination.

Starting points

- *Dracula* combines myths and history with imagination to create its story. Does this help to make it more believable? Which is more important – imagination, tradition, or fact?

- In its time, *Dracula* was a very modern novel, describing many of the latest technologies in the story. If Bram Stoker was writing today, what new technologies might he include? How might they influence the outcome?

- In any confrontation between the modern world and an older power, is the modern world certain to win? What advantages does the 'modern world' have, and what might help the 'older power'? Can you think of any other examples of this sort of confrontation, in fiction or in the real world?

Themes

Bram Stoker addresses all these themes in *Dracula*. What do you think he is saying about them? Do you agree with him?

- modernity and its consequences
- salvation and damnation
- science versus superstition
- power and hierarchy

Style

Can you find paragraphs containing examples of the following?

- descriptions of setting and atmosphere
- the use of a very simple sentence to achieve a particular effect
- the use of imagery to enhance description
- emotive writing

Look closely at how these paragraphs are written. What do you notice? Can you write a paragraph in the same style?